Barclay and Berk Builders
A PARABLE

Retold by BEVERLEY RAYNER

Illustrated by JAMES HENSMAN

Brought to you by Gulliver S. Gull

To Hayley

God Bless you

B Rayner

Barclay & Berk Builders: A Parable
Copyright ©2021 Beverley Rayner

Published by Castle Quay Books
Burlington, Ontario, Canada and Jupiter, Florida, U.S.A.
416-573-3249 | info@castlequaybooks.com | www.castlequaybooks.com

Printed in Canada.

Illustrations by James Hensman
Cover design and book interior by James Hensman

978-1-988928-55-5 Soft Cover
978-1-988928-56-2 E-book

Library and Archives Canada Cataloguing in Publication

Title: Barclay and Berk builders : a parable / retold by Beverley Rayner ; illustrated by James
    Hensman.
Other titles: Adaptation of (Work): Bible. Matthew, VII, 24-27.
Names: Rayner, Beverley, author. | Hensman, James, illustrator.
Description: Adaptation of: Matthew 7:24–27.
Identifiers: Canadiana (print) 20210297654 | Canadiana (ebook) 20210297662 | ISBN 9781988928555
    (softcover) | ISBN 9781988928562 (EPUB)
Subjects: LCSH: House built upon a rock (Parable)—Juvenile literature. | LCSH: Bible stories—New
    Testament.
Classification: LCC BT378.H68 R39 2021 | DDC j226.2/09505—dc23

CASTLE QUAY BOOKS

DEDICATED TO TORIN

Future digger and builder of all things wonderful.

Unless the LORD builds the house, the builders labour in vain. PSALM 127:1 NIV

Dedicated to the memory of the two people who started directing my creativity: Shirley Hensman and Lorraine Sells. — *James Hensman*

Barclay and Berk are builders, both solid and firm, with bulging biceps. Together they can build just about anything—from sandboxes to bike ramps, tree houses, and jungle gyms. They do it all. But right now, they each need a house.

Barclay is thinking about the big house he wants to build. It will have large windows, so sunshine slips into every corner, a wooden entrance with seven steps leading up to a bright yellow door, and maybe even a turret on top!

5

Berk thinks that his house will have a stone fireplace to keep everyone warm in winter and a swinging cat door. Kitty can share it with Trip, the dog. Then they can go outside and come back in whenever they like.

Berk's wife says she will weave a colourful welcome mat.

Barclay and Berk know a lot about building. They each have a red metal toolbox with all kinds of helpful tools: hammer, nails, screwdrivers, chisels, clamps, and so much more. Barclay's favourite tool is his nail gun, which makes a loud snapping sound. He squeezes the trigger, and forced air drives the nails into the wood: sch-wack; and it's done!

Barclay finds a sunny place for his house. "This is the ideal place for me," he decides, stretching out his arms and gazing around as a breeze ruffles his hair. He imagines sitting on his front deck, licking an orange popsicle—his favourite—and watching seagulls swoop over the rolling white foam on the water.

"What about you, Berk?" Barclay calls. "Have you found a plot of land to build on?"

"No, not yet," Berk replies. He then struts about, his head low, standing high above Barclay on top of some sandy dunes where long, tufty grasses sway. Berk digs the heel of his work boot into the soft earth.

Barclay runs up to stand beside him. "How about right here?" he suggests.

"No, no," mutters Berk. "It's not quite right."

The next day, Barclay is up early in the morning with the birds and driving his rickety truck. The truck is so dirty that it's difficult to tell what colour might be under all the grime. Barclay is hauling a big excavator that's strapped down tight to a trailer. "This is a perfect day for digging!" Barclay announces, to no one in particular. He quickly sets to work.

Berk watches from a safe distance. The excavator rumbles to life and begins to scoop huge buckets of sandy soil; then, swinging a long jerky neck, it dumps dirt onto a pile.

Berk ponders the idea of building next to Barclay where there's a great ocean view.

As the sun drops down, and the heat of a summer sun spills amber into the water, Barclay shuts off the excavator. All is quiet. "Phew!" he says, wiping a sweaty forehead with his sleeve. "I'm glad that's done! Digging is not my favourite thing to do, even with an excavator. Digging is not my favourite!"

Berk has finally found a place for his house: on top of a rocky cliff.

"Are you sure?" asks Barclay. "It's rather windy up here." Berk is sure.

He arrives with a jackhammer and a rock drill, to break up the rock. The drill will bore down deep. It's a very noisy job, and after a day's work, Berk feels like he's been rattled and shaken from head to toe.

Barclay was busy all day. The framing of his house is done! But the loud clattering, bashing, and whizzing sounds have scared the birds away.

14

With a plumb line and a keen eye, Berk constructs concrete footings deep into the rock. He is building a foundation for a sturdy base underneath his house. Berk mutters to himself, "Not quite right," every time his measurements are not equal. He keeps working until everything is level.

Barclay has stacked up an enormous pile of lumber in all shapes and sizes. His leather tool belt is very handy when it comes to building something big.

Two walls, with gaping holes like eye sockets, stand ready for windows.

"Look at my house!" Barclay says. He is excited. Berk looks up from where he's kneeling on the rock. His knees hurt. Berk's concrete footings are taking a long time. He views Barclay's superstructure down below.

"What a splendid house you will have!" Berk says.

Berk is finally ready to build upwards with some sturdy timber posts. They are heavy, but he is strong. Still, it takes all Berk's strength to haul and place the posts just where they need to be. Then he measures all around. Oops! One post is not quite right. Berk will make sure that it is.

Barclay is singing while he works. He's up on the roof, hammering wood shingles and using his nail gun. Sch-wack, sch-wack, and another one is done. Time for the next!

Barclay and Berk work all summer. Just as the leaves fine-tune their colours to lacy shades of golden bronze, and the geese honk farewell overhead, Barclay paints his door a brilliant bright yellow! His house is finished!

What a magnificent house! There are big windows all around with sunshine slipping into every corner, a wooden entrance with seven steps leading up to a bright yellow door, and there's even a turret. Barclay has yellow paint in his hair and on his elbows, but he doesn't mind. Tomorrow he will move in.

Berk is gathering large stones for his fireplace. His house is just big enough for two and the pets. He needs a roof and a chimney. He still has a lot of work to do, but Berk doesn't hurry. He wants his house to be just right.

The days are getting shorter, and there's frost on Barclay's rooftop in the mornings.

"Brrr." Berk shivers one morning. He is glad that his work is almost finished. When it gets too cold to be outside, the inside of his house will be warm and cozy.

Barclay and Berk are finally finished with the building of their homes. Time to take a vacation. Berk visits Barclay at his house, where they play Scrabble. Then Barclay visits Berk at his house, where they sit by the fire roasting chestnuts. Berk's wife sits nearby, knitting in her armchair.

Just before Christmas, a fierce wind blows in from the sea, tossing the ocean waves and hurling them to the shore with the strength of an angry giant. Ships sail fast for safe harbours, as flags snap furiously and trees double over. Berk peers out his window into the dark night. All he can see is a soft golden glow from the windows of Barclay's house.

22

Smoke billows from Berk's chimney, whipping away to sea. Then a sudden gust of wind shakes his house with a deep shudder. It's a windy night tonight, Berk thinks.

"Come away from the window, my dear," says Berk's wife. "I've made mugs of hot chocolate with mini marshmallows on top. We can sit by the fireplace while sipping our hot chocolate."

Barclay's windows rattle. The fierce wind is turning into a mighty storm. Barclay paces the floor. He hears a ripping sound; just a loose shingle from the roof, no doubt. No problem. Tomorrow he will fix it.

The winter winds howl as the heavy rain beats against the windows. Lightning snakes and cracks across the dark night, and the heavy rumble of thunder grows ever closer. Barclay doesn't like storms.

Suddenly, a deafening boom thunders overhead, and Barclay jumps up, startled. There's a groaning sound coming from the roof. The floor beneath Barclay's feet begins to shift. A massive crash might happen at any moment! Barclay doesn't wait a minute longer. He grabs his raincoat and Wellington boots. Then, holding onto his hat, he charges out into the storm.

Kitty yawns and stretches a little closer to the fireplace at Berk's house. Trip growls, just once, as a faint knocking is heard at the door. Trip jumps up and races for the cat door flap and disappears.

"Good gracious," Berk says. "Someone at the door in a storm like this? Who can it be?"

Berk opens the door and hugs his friend. "Oh, what a night! Come in, Barclay, old friend. Tomorrow we'll check the damage."

Barclay enters, soaking wet and dripping all over the welcome mat. Trip licks his hand and whines as they hear the moaning of the winds, followed by a shattering sound. Barclay can't see in the darkness, but he knows what is happening. His house is falling apart.

Even though Berk's house is only big enough for two, there is still room for Barclay to sleep by the fireplace. Berk has a spare pair of slippers and some rocket pyjamas.

Barclay can't sleep. Snuggled in a cozy blanket that belongs to Trip, he stares at the warm red glow of embers.

The following morning, there is a peaceful hush over the waters. Barclay and Berk stand silently gazing at the heap of rubble, broken glass, and twisted wood that was once Barclay's splendid house.

Among the wreckage, they find the yellow door. "I didn't build a strong foundation," Barclay wails. "Everything came crashing down."

Berk gives him a comforting pat on the back. "You can build again," he says. "I'll help."

"But that will take too long," Barclay moans. "All that's left is my yellow door."

"It will take time, that's true," Berk replies. "But together, we can build a strong foundation. When we're finished, your new home will be just right!"

Jesus said: *"Therefore everyone who hears these words of mine and puts them into practice is like a wise man who built his house on the rock. The rain came down, the streams rose, and the winds blew and beat against that house, yet it did not fall, because it had its foundation on the rock. But everyone who hears these words of mine and does not put them into practice is like a foolish man who built his house on sand. The rain came down, the streams rose, and the winds blew and beat against that house, and it fell with a great crash."* MATTHEW 7:24-27 NIV

CASTLE QUAY BOOKS

WWW.CASTLEQUAYBOOKS.COM

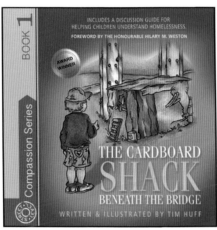

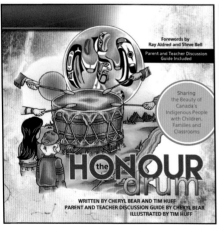